Homebody

Homebody

19093-92

by Joyce McDonald

illustrated by Karl Swanson

G.P. Putnam's Sons   New York

Text copyright © 1991 by Joyce McDonald
Illustrations copyright © 1991 by Karl Swanson
All rights reserved. This book, or parts thereof, may not be reproduced
in any form without permission in writing from the publisher.
G. P. Putnam's Sons, a division of The Putnam & Grosset Book Group,
200 Madison Avenue, New York, NY 10016
Published simultaneously in Canada
Printed in Hong Kong by South China Printing Co. (1988) Ltd.
Designed by Jean Weiss

Library of Congress Cataloging-in-Publication Data
McDonald, Joyce. Homebody / by Joyce McDonald;
illustrations by Karl Swanson. p.   cm.
Summary: Abandoned when her family moves away,
a thin gray cat persists in remaining near the house
which she considers home, and she is eventually
rewarded for her faithfulness.
[1. Cats—Fiction.   2. Dwellings—Fiction.]   I. Swanson, Karl W., ill.   II. Title.
PZ7.M14817Ho   1991   89-29602 CIP AC   [E]—dc20
ISBN 0-399-21939-0
1   3   5   7   9   10   8   6   4   2
First Impression

This story is dedicated to the homeless
and the uprooted, animal and human alike,
and to the gray cat on Stark Road.

And above all, to my parents—JM

To my father, Howard Swanson—KS

One moonless night, while the dark silence held their secret, the Peeble family stole away from their falling-down house. They did not tell the landlord they were going. But they did leave him a present. A mountain of trash so high it was almost as tall as Mr. Peeble. They also left behind a dog with fur the color of a penny and one thin gray cat.

The cat waited. And waited.

The Peebles did not return.

But the gray cat did not leave. Home was home. And that was that.

The cat hunted mice in a nearby field, without much success. And when the hunger was more than she could bear, she munched a beetle or two. The old dog tried hunting rabbits, but he had forgotten how to hunt and so, like the cat, grew thin.

Sometimes, when she was lonely, the cat poked and pawed about the mountain of trash. She would pull a broken water pistol or a torn teddy bear from the rubble. The toys reminded her of the Peeble children. The cat curled up with her treasures and waited.

And waited.

But the Peebles never came.

Then one warm August morning, a few weeks later, a man named Joe Budd drove a shiny pickup truck into the driveway. He was the new owner of the falling-down house.

Joe stood with his hands on his hips and shook his head. He shook his head at the mountain of trash and at the torn screens. He shook his head at the roofing shingles that had tumbled to the ground, and at the uncut grass and weeds. Joe's plan was to fix up the old house and sell it. He could see he had his work cut out for him.

The gray cat hid in the nearby bushes with the dog. They watched Joe load some of the trash into his truck.

Suddenly something brushed the cat's fur. It was the penny-colored dog. He walked slowly from their hiding place, his head bent low. Joe stopped working and stared. When the dog was only a few feet away, Joe hunkered down and held out his hand. He petted the nameless dog and felt how thin he was.

"Well," Joe said, "where did you come from?"

As if he understood the man's question, the dog lumbered over to the porch and flopped down in front of the door. Joe looked surprised, and then concerned.

"Did they leave you behind, old friend?" he asked. "How would you like to come home with me?"

The dog wagged his tail in answer and climbed into Joe's truck. From the bushes, the gray cat watched her friend ride away. But *she* was not about to leave. Because home was home. And that was that.

Almost every day Joe came to work on the house. And the dog, whom he had named Sam, came with him. Sometimes Joe brought his young son, Brian. Together they filled a big dumpster with the mountain of trash, while the gray cat looked on from her hiding place.

On other days, Joe ripped off the old shingles and replaced them with new ones. He repaired the torn screens. Brian helped to gather the old shingles from the ground. Each evening, after Joe and Brian and the dog had left, the gray cat crawled from behind the bushes and stubbornly curled into sleep on the porch of the falling-down house. She was going to stay, even if the house fell down around her ears. Because home was home. And that was that.

One morning, on her way to work, Mrs. Grundy from across the street noticed the gray cat sitting all alone. She tried to get the cat to come live with her. But the cat would not budge. After that, Mrs. Grundy brought food to her every day.

Once, as she was crossing the road with a bowl of food, she met Joe Budd and Brian. They looked surprised to see Mrs. Grundy carrying a bowl of cat food to their house.

"For me?" Joe asked.

Mrs. Grundy chuckled. "For the gray cat," she said. "But I can bring you some too, if you'd like."

"What gray cat?" Brian asked.

Mrs. Grundy told them all about the cat. Joe listened and looked around. He did not see a gray cat anywhere. Still, he said that Mrs. Grundy was welcome to bring food whenever she pleased.

Fall was coming and the nights were growing cool. One stormy evening, Mrs. Grundy brought a little dog house, which had once belonged to her beagle, to the falling-down house. As the wind and rain whipped about her ears, she set the little house on the porch and stuffed it with an old, worn blanket. The gray cat weaved about her legs as Mrs. Grundy worked, and purred as if she understood.

The next day Mrs. Grundy told Joe about the little house. Even though he had never seen the gray cat, he thanked Mrs. Grundy for the cat's shelter. After that, Mrs. Grundy stopped every evening on her way home from work and flashed her car headlights on the little house to make sure the gray cat was all right.

Other men began coming to the house. Men with hammers and saws. And every day the cat watched them from her hiding place in the bushes. They tore down part of the porch, but not the part where the cat's house sat.

More men came. Men with machines. They made a lot of noise and when they were done, half the concrete slab where the porch had been was gone. Nothing was left but a large, deep hole. But half the concrete slab remained. The half with the gray cat's house.

Still the men came. They hammered and sawed as the cat looked on from the bushes. They worked all around the little house. But they never disturbed it. And when they were done, a whole new room stood where half the old porch had been. But not the half with the gray cat's house.

Every night, after Joe and the men had gone, the gray cat crept back to the little house and circled herself into the worn blanket. And every morning, after breakfast with Mrs. Grundy, she stretched her ears to listen for the sound of the men and the trucks. When the sound reached her, she fled to her hiding place. But she never ran far. Home was home. And that was that.

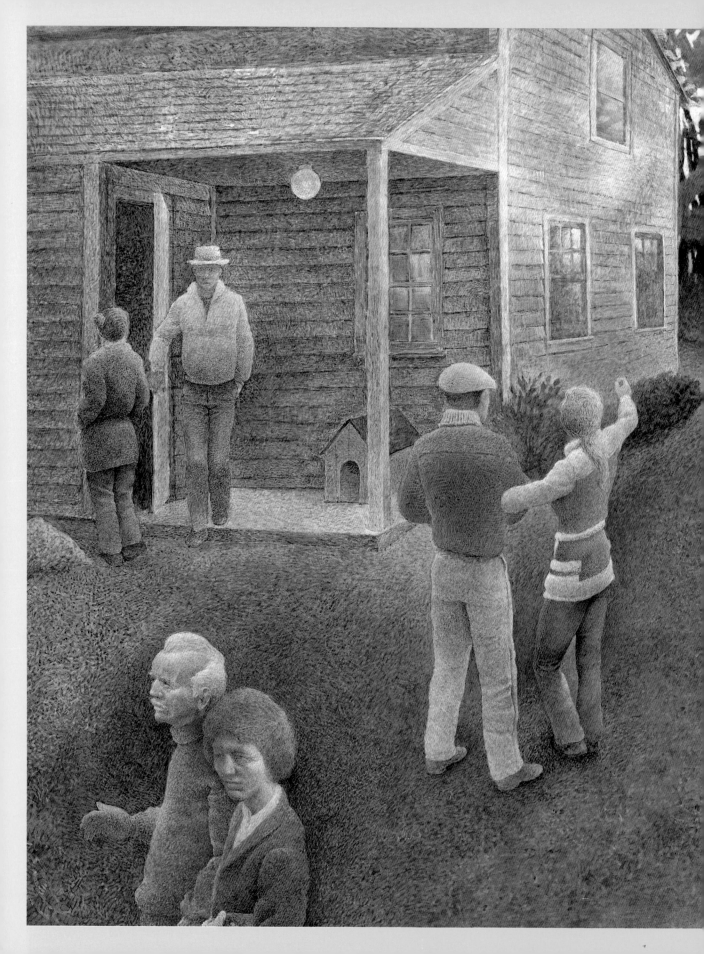

Then one autumn day Joe Budd put a "For Sale" sign in the front yard. More people began coming to the house. People who went about frowning and nodding. The gray cat looked on. She did not know the people were thinking of buying the house.

On one frosty, windy night, before they left for home, Joe and Brian rested a large, flat piece of wood against the side of the porch to shelter a cat they had never seen. But they knew there was a cat hiding about somewhere, even though they had never met her. And they wanted to help.

After many weeks, the house was no longer a falling-down house. It had a new roof and a new room, and new windows and screens. It had new carpets and wallpaper, and it had been painted blue.

Joe and Brian stood before the house and admired their work. Joe was so pleased with his new house that he brought his wife to see it a few days later. And she agreed. It was indeed a fine house. When they left, Joe took the "For Sale" sign with him.

Just before the first winter snow, the Budds moved into the blue house. It was not what Joe had started out to do, but he liked the house too much to sell it to anyone else.

The next morning when Mrs. Grundy brought the bowl of food, there sat the gray cat on top of the little house. The cat licked her paws and watched Joe and Brian paint her house with leftover blue paint. It looked just like the big house. Sam the dog lay by Joe's feet. He seemed happy to be home.

"Well," Mrs. Grundy said, pointing to the gray cat. "I see you've finally met."

"Oh, yes," Joe said. He stroked the cat's fur and scratched her behind the ears. The gray cat purred and purred. "She's decided to let us live here with her."

"Ah," Mrs. Grundy said. "Quite a homebody, that one."

"Homebody. That's a good name for her," Brian said. And Joe agreed.

The gray cat stretched and yawned as if she knew what Mrs. Grundy said was true. She would never leave this house. Not ever. Because, after all, home was home. And that was that.